D1647124

Anthony is a popular and prolific children's writer whose books now sell in more than a dozen countries around the world. He has won numerous prizes for his books, which include *Stormbreaker* (shortlisted for the 2000 Children's Book Award) and its sequels *Point Blanc*, *Skeleton Key*, *Eagle Strike*, *Scorpia* and *Ark Angel* about reluctant teenage MI6 spy Alex Rider; *Groosham Grange* and its sequel *The Unholy Grail*; *Granny* (shortlisted for the 1994 Children's Book Award); and the Diamond Brothers trilogy – *The Falcon's Malteser* (which has been filmed with the title *Just Ask for Diamond*), followed by *South by South East* (which was dramatized in six parts on TV) and *Public Enemy Number Two* – to which *The Blurred Man* and two other short novels, *I Know What You Did Last Wednesday* and *The French Confection*, have been added.

Anthony also writes extensively for TV, with credits including the hit series *Murder in Mind*, as well as *Foyle's War*, *Midsomer Murders*, *Poirot* and *Murder Most Horrid*, and he has been described by the *Radio Times* as "a one-man crime-wave". He is married to the television producer Jill Green and lives in north London with their two children, Nicholas and Cassian, and their dog, Unlucky.

You can find out more about Anthony Horowitz and his books by visiting his website at
www.anthonyhorowitz.com

Other Diamond Brothers books

The Falcon's Malteser

South by South East

Public Enemy Number Two

The French Confection

I Know What You Did Last Wednesday

The Alex Rider books

Stormbreaker

Point Blanc

Skeleton Key

Eagle Strike

Scorpia

Ark Angel

Other books by the same author

The Devil and His Boy

Granny

Groosham Grange

The Switch

The Unholy Grail

ANTHONY HOROWITZ

WALKER BOOKS
AND SUBSIDIARIES

LONDON · BOSTON · SYDNEY · AUCKLAND

First published 2002 by Walker Books Ltd
87 Vauxhall Walk, London SE11 5HJ

This edition published 2003

6 8 10 9 7 5

Text © 2002 Anthony Horowitz
Cover illustration © 2002 Phil Schramm

This book has been typeset in Sabon

Printed in Great Britain by Cox & Wyman Ltd, Reading, Berkshire

British Library Cataloguing in Publication Data:
a catalogue record for this book
is available from the British Library

ISBN-13: 978-0-7445-9066-1
ISBN-10: 0-7445-9066-3
www.walkerbooks.co.uk

CONTENTS

1	The Pen Pal	7
2	Dead Man's Footsteps	22
3	A Night at the Circus	40
4	The Real Lenny Smile	57
5	The Big Wheel	69

THE PEN PAL

I knew the American was going to mean trouble, the moment he walked through the door. He only made it on the third attempt. It was eleven o'clock in the morning but clearly he'd been drinking since breakfast – and breakfast had probably come out of a bottle too. The smell of whisky was so strong it made my eyes water. Drunk at eleven o'clock! I didn't like to think what it was doing to him, but if I'd been his liver I'd have been applying for a transplant.

He managed to find a seat and slumped into it. The funny thing was, he was quite smartly dressed: a suit and a tie that looked expensive. I got the feeling straight away that this was someone with money. He was wearing gold-rimmed glasses, and as far as I could tell we were talking real gold. He was about forty years old, with hair that was just turning grey and eyes that were just turning yellow. That must have been the whisky. He took out a cigarette and lit it. Blue smoke filled the room. This man would not have been a good advertisement for the National Health Service.

"My name is Carter," he said at last. He spoke with an American accent. "Joe Carter. I just got in from Chicago. And I've got a problem."

"I can see that," I muttered.

He glanced at me with one eye. The other eye looked somewhere over my shoulder. "Who are you?" he demanded.

"I'm Nick Diamond."

"I don't need a smart-arse kid. I'm looking for a private detective."

"That's him over there," I said, indicating the desk and my big brother, Tim.

"You want a coffee, Mr Carver?" Tim asked.

"It's not Carver. It's Carter. With a 't'," the American growled.

"I'm out of tea. How about a hot chocolate?"

"I don't want a hot anything!" Carter sucked on the cigarette. "I want help. I want to hire you. What do you charge?"

Tim stared. Although it was hard to believe, the American was offering him money. This was something that didn't happen often. Tim hadn't really made any money since he'd worked as a policeman, and even then the police dogs had earned more than him. At least they'd bitten the right man. As a private detective, Tim had been a total calamity. I'd helped him solve one or two cases, but most of the time I was stuck at school. Right now it was the week of half-term – six weeks before Christmas, and once again it didn't look like our stockings were going to be full. Unless you're talking holes. Tim had just seven pence left in his bank account. We'd written a begging letter to our mum and dad in Australia but were still saving up for the stamp.

I coughed and Tim jerked upright in his chair, trying to look businesslike. "You need a private detective?" he said. "Fine. That's me. But it'll cost you fifty pounds a day, plus expenses."

"You take traveller's cheques?"

"That depends on the traveller."

"I don't have cash."

"Traveller's cheques are fine," I said.

Joe Carter pulled out a bundle of blue traveller's cheques, then fumbled for a pen. For a moment I was worried that he'd be too drunk to sign them. But somehow he managed to scribble his name five times on the dotted lines, and slid the cheques across. "All right," he said. "That's five hundred dollars."

"Five hundred dollars!" Tim squeaked. The last time he'd had that much money in his hand he'd been playing Monopoly. "Five hundred dollars...?"

"About three hundred and fifty pounds," I told him.

Carter nodded. "Right. So now let me tell you where I'm coming from."

"I thought you were coming from Chicago," Tim said.

"I mean, let me tell you my problem. I got into England last Tuesday, a little less than a week ago. I'm staying in a hotel in the West End. The Ritz."

"You'd be crackers to stay anywhere else," Tim said.

"Yeah." Carter stubbed his cigarette out in the ashtray. Except we didn't have an ashtray. The smell of burning wood rose from the surface of Tim's desk. "I'm a writer, Mr Diamond. You may have read some of my books."

That was unlikely – unless he wrote children's books. Tim had recently started *Just William* for the fourth time.

"I'm pretty well-known in the States," Carter continued. "*The Big Bullet. Death in the Afternoon. Rivers of Blood.* Those are some of my titles."

"Romances?" Tim asked.

"No. They're crime novels. I'm successful. I make a ton of money out of my writing – but, you know, I believe in sharing it around. I'm not married. I don't have kids. So I give it to charity. All sorts of charities. Mostly back home in the States, of course, but also in other parts of the world."

I wondered if he'd like to make a donation to the bankrupt brothers of dumb detectives, a little charity of my own. But I didn't say anything.

"Now, a couple of years back I heard of a charity operating here in England," he went on. "It was called Dream Time and I kind of liked the sound of it. Dream Time was there to help kids get more out of life. It bought computers and books and special equipment for schools. It also bought schools. It helped train kids who wanted to get into sport. Or who wanted to paint. Or who had never travelled." Carter glanced at me. "How old are you, son?" he asked.

"Fourteen," I said.

"I bet you make wishes sometimes."

"Yes. But unfortunately Tim is still here."

"Dream Time would help you. They make wishes come true." Carter reached into his pocket and took out a hip-flask. He unscrewed it and threw it back. It seemed to do him good. "A little Scotch," he explained.

"I thought you were American," Tim said.

"I gave Dream Time two million dollars of my money because I believed in them!" Carter exclaimed. "Most of all, I believed in the man

11

behind Dream Time. He was a saint. He was a lovely guy. His name was Lenny Smile."

I noticed that Carter was talking about Smile in the past tense. I was beginning to see the way this conversation might be going.

"What can I tell you about Lenny?" Carter went on. "Like me, he never married. He didn't have a big house or a fancy car or anything like that. In fact he lived in a small apartment in a part of London called Battersea. Dream Time had been his idea and he worked for it seven days a week, three hundred and sixty-five days a year. Lenny loved leap years because then he could work three hundred and sixty-six days a year. That was the sort of man he was. When I heard about him, I knew I had to support his work. So I gave him a quarter of a million dollars. And then another quarter. And so on..."

"So what's the problem, Mr Starter?" Tim asked. "You want your money back?"

"Hell, no! Let me explain. I loved this guy Lenny. I felt like I'd known him all my life. But recently, I decided we ought to meet."

"You'd never met him?"

"No. We were pen pals. We exchanged letters. Lots of letters – and e-mails. He used to write to me and I'd write back. That's how I got to know him. But I was busy with my work. And he was busy with his. We never met. We never even spoke. And then, recently,

I suddenly realized I needed a break. I'd been working so hard, I decided to come over to England and have a vacation."

"Wouldn't you have preferred a holiday?" Tim asked.

"I wrote to Lenny and told him I'd like to meet him. He was really pleased to hear from me. He said he wanted to show me all the work he'd been doing. All the children who'd benefited from the money I'd sent. I was really looking forward to the trip. He was going to meet me at Heathrow Airport."

"How would you know what he looked like if you'd never met?" I asked.

Carter blushed. "Well, I did sometimes wonder about that. So once I'd arranged to come I asked him to send me a photograph of himself."

He reached into his jacket and took out a photograph. He handed it to me.

The picture showed a man standing in front of a café in what could have been London or Paris. It was hard to be sure. I could see the words CAFÉ DEBUSSY written on the windows. But the man himself was harder to make out. Whoever had taken the photograph should have asked Dream Time for a new camera. It was completely out of focus. I could just make out a man in a black suit with a full-length coat. He was wearing gloves and a hat. But his face was a blur. He might have had dark hair.

I think he was smiling. There was a cat sitting on the pavement between his legs, and the cat was easier to make out than he was.

"It's not a very good picture," I said.

"I know." Carter took it back. "Lenny was a very shy person. He didn't even sign his letters. That's how shy he was. He told me that he didn't like going out very much. You see, there's something else you need to know about him. He was sick. He had this illness ... some kind of allergy."

"Was Algy his doctor?" Tim asked.

"No, no. An allergy. It meant he reacted to things. Peanuts, for example. They made him swell up. And he hated publicity. There have been a couple of stories about him in the newspapers, but he wouldn't give interviews and there were never any photographs. The Queen wanted to knight him, apparently, but sadly he was also allergic to queens. All that mattered to him was his work ... Dream Time ... helping kids. Anyway, meeting him was going to be the biggest moment of my life... I was as excited as a schoolboy."

As excited as a schoolboy? Obviously Carter had never visited my school.

"Only when I got to Heathrow, Lenny wasn't there. He wasn't in London either. I never got to meet him. And you know why?"

I knew why. But I waited for Lenny to tell me.

"Lenny was buried the day before I arrived," Carter said.

"Buried?" Tim exclaimed. "Why?"

"Because it was his funeral, Mr Diamond!" Carter lit another cigarette. "He was dead. And that's why I'm here. I want you to find out what happened."

"What did happen?" I asked.

"Well, like I told you, I arrived here at Heathrow last Tuesday. All I could think about was meeting Lenny Smile, shaking that man's hand and telling him just how much he meant to me. When he didn't show up, I didn't even check into my hotel. I went straight to the offices of Dream Time. And that was when they told me..."

"Who told you?" I asked.

"A man called Hoover. Rodney Hoover..."

"That name sucks," Tim said.

Carter ignored him. "He worked for Lenny, helping him run Dream Time. There's another assistant there too, called Fiona Lee. She's very posh. Upper-class, you know? They have an office just the other side of Battersea Bridge. It's right over the café you saw in that photo. Anyway, it seems that just a few days after I e-mailed Lenny to tell him I was coming, he got killed in a horrible accident, crossing the road."

"He fell down a manhole?" Tim asked.

"No, Mr Diamond. He got run over.

Hoover and Lee actually saw it happen. If they hadn't been there, the police wouldn't even have known it was Lenny."

"Why is that?"

"Because he was run over by a steamroller." Carter shuddered. Tim shivered. Even the desk light flickered. I had to admit, it was a pretty horrible way to go. "He was flattened," the American went on. "They told me that the ambulance people had to fold him before they could get him onto a stretcher. He was buried last week. At Brompton Cemetery, near Fulham."

Brompton. That was where the master criminal known as the Falcon had been buried too. Tim and I had gone to the cemetery at the end of our first ever case*. We were lucky we weren't still there.

"This guy Rodney Hoover tells me he's winding down Dream Time," Carter went on. "He says it wouldn't be the same without Lenny, and he doesn't have the heart to go on without him. I had a long talk with him in his office and I have to tell you ... I didn't like it."

"You don't think it's a nice office?" Tim asked.

"I think something strange is going on."

Tim blinked. "What exactly do you think is strange?"

Carter almost choked on his cigarette. "Goddammit!" he yelled. "You don't think

* See *The Falcon's Malteser*

16

there's anything unusual in a guy getting run over by a steamroller? It happens in the middle of the night and just a few days before he's due to have a meeting with someone who's given him two million dollars! And the next thing you hear, the charity he'd set up is suddenly shutting down! You don't think that's all a little strange?"

"It's certainly strange that it happened in the middle of the night," Tim agreed. "Why wasn't he in bed?"

"I don't know why he wasn't in bed – but I'll tell you this: I think he was murdered. A man doesn't walk in front of a steamroller. But maybe he's pushed. Maybe this has got something to do with money ... my money. Maybe somebody didn't want us to meet! I know that if I was writing this as a novel, that's the way it would turn out. Anyway, there are plenty of private detectives in London. If you're not interested, I can find someone who is. So are you going to look into this for me or not?"

Tim glanced at the traveller's cheques. He scooped them up. "Don't worry, Mr Carpark," he said. "I'll find the truth. The only question is – where do I find you?"

"I'm still at the Ritz," Carter said. "Ask for Room 8."

"I'll ask for you," Tim said. "But if you're out, I suppose the room-mate will have to do."

*   *   *

We changed the traveller's cheques into cash and blew some of it on the first decent meal we'd had in a week. Tim was in a good mood. He even let me have a pudding.

"I can't believe it!" he exclaimed, as the waitress served us two ice-cream sundaes. The service in the restaurant was so slow that they were more like Mondays by the time they arrived. "Three hundred and fifty pounds! That's more money than I've earned in a month."

"It's more money than you've earned in a year," I reminded him.

"And all because some crazy American thinks his pen pal was murdered."

"How do you know he wasn't?"

"Intuition." Tim tapped the side of his nose. "I can't explain it to you, kid. I've just got a feeling."

"You've also got ice-cream on your nose," I said.

After lunch we took the bus over to Fulham. I don't know why Tim decided to start in Brompton Cemetery. Maybe he wanted to visit it for old times' sake. It had been more than a year since we'd last been there, but the place hadn't changed. And why should it have? I doubted any of the residents had complained. None of them would have had the energy to redecorate. The gravestones were as weird as ever, some of them like Victorian telephone boxes, others like miniature castles with doors fastened by rusting chains and padlocks. You'd have needed a skeleton key to open them. The place was divided into separate areas: some old, some more modern. There must have been thousands of people there but of course none of them offered to show us the way to Smile's grave. We had to find it on our own.

It took us about an hour. It was on the edge of the cemetery, overshadowed by the football stadium next door. We might never have found it except that the grave had been recently dug. That was one clue. And there were fresh flowers. That was another. Smile had been given a lot of flowers. In fact, if he hadn't been dead he could have opened a florist's. I read the gravestone:

LENNY SMILE
April 31st 1955 – November 11th 2001
A Wonderful Man, Called to Rest.

We stood in silence for a moment. It seemed too bad that someone who had done so much for children all over the world hadn't even made it to fifty. I glanced at the biggest bunch of flowers on the grave. There was a card attached. It was signed in green ink, *With love, from Rodney Hoover and Fiona Lee.*

There was a movement on the other side of

the cemetery. I had thought we were alone when we arrived, but now I realized that there was a man, watching us. He was a long way away, standing behind one of the taller gravestones, but even at that distance I thought there was something familiar about him, and I found myself shivering without quite knowing why. He was wearing a full-length coat with gloves and a hat. I couldn't make out his face. From this distance, it was just a blur. And that was when I realized. I knew exactly where I'd seen him before. I started forward, running towards him. At that moment he turned round and hurried off, moving away from me.

"Nick!" Tim called out.

I ignored him and ran through the cemetery. There was a gravestone in the way and I jumped over it. Maybe that wasn't a respectful thing to do but I wasn't feeling exactly religious. I reached the main path and sprinted forward. I didn't know if Tim was following me or not. I didn't care.

The northern gates of the cemetery opened onto Old Brompton Road. I burst out and stood there, catching my breath. It came as a shock, coming from the land of the dead into that of the living, with buses and cabs roaring past. An old woman, wrapped in three cardigans, was selling flowers right next to the gate. Business can't have been good. Half the flowers were as dead as the people they were meant for. I went over to her.

"Excuse me..." I said. "Did someone just come out through this gate?"

The old woman shook her head. "No, dear. I didn't see anyone."

"Are you sure? A man in a long coat. He was wearing a hat..."

"People don't come out of the cemetery," the old woman said. "When they get there, they stay there."

A moment later, Tim proved her wrong by appearing at the gate. "What is it, Nick?" he asked.

I looked up and down the pavement. There was nobody in sight. Had I imagined it? No. I was certain. The man I had seen in Joe Carter's photograph had been in the cemetery less than a minute ago. Once I'd spotted him, he had run away.

But that was impossible, wasn't it?

If it was Lenny Smile that I had just seen, then who was buried in the grave?

DEAD MAN'S FOOTSTEPS

We began our search for Lenny Smile the next day – at the Battersea offices of the charity he had created.

I knew the building, of course, from the photograph Carter had shown us. Dream Time's headquarters were above the Café Debussy, which was in the middle of a row of half-derelict shops a few minutes' walk from the River Thames. It was hard to believe that a charity worth millions of pounds could operate from such a small, shabby place. But maybe that was the point. Maybe they didn't want to spend the money they raised on plush offices in the West End. It's the same reason why Oxfam shops always look so run down. That way they can afford another ox.

But the inside of Dream Time was something else. The walls had been knocked through to create an open-plan area with carpets that reached up to your ankles and leather furniture you couldn't believe had started life as a cow. The light fittings looked Italian. Low lighting at high prices. There were framed pictures on the walls, of smiling children from around the world: Asia, Africa, Europe and so on. The receptionist was smiling too. We already knew that the place was being shut down, and I could see that she didn't have a lot to do. She'd just finished polishing her nails when we walked in. While we were waiting she started polishing her teeth.

At last a door opened and Fiona Lee walked in. At least, I guessed it must be her. We'd rung that morning and made an appointment. She was tall and slim, with her dark hair tied back in such a vicious bun that you'd expect it to explode at any moment. She had the looks of a model, but I'm talking the Airfix variety. All plastic. Her make-up was perfect. Her clothes were perfect. Everything about her was perfect, down to the last detail. Either she spent hours getting ready every morning, or she slept hanging in the wardrobe so that she didn't rumple her skin.

"Good morning," she said. Joe Carter had been right about her. She had such a posh accent that when she spoke you heard every letter. "My name is Fiona Lee."

We introduced ourselves.

She looked from Tim to me and back again.

She didn't seem impressed. "Do come in," she said. She spun round on her heel. With heels like hers I was surprised she didn't drill a hole in the floor.

We followed her down a corridor lined with more smiling kids. At the end was a door that led to an office on a corner, with views of Battersea Park one way and the Thames the other. Rodney Hoover was sitting behind a desk cluttered with papers and half-dead potted plants, talking on the telephone. An ugly desk for a very ugly man. Both of them looked like they were made of wood. He was running to fat and might have been a little less fat if he'd taken up running. He had drooping shoulders and jet black hair that oozed oil. He was wearing an old-fashioned suit that was too small for him and glasses that were too big. As he finished his call, I noticed that he had horrible teeth. In fact the last time I'd seen teeth like that, they'd been in a dog. Mrs Lee signalled and we sat down. Hoover hung up. He had been speaking with a strong accent that could have been Russian or German. I noticed he had bad breath. No wonder the potted plants on his desk were wilting.

"Good morning," he said.

"This is Tim Diamond, Mr Hoover," Mrs Lee said. She pronounced his name *Teem Daymond*. "He telephoned this morning."

"Oh yes. Yes!" Hoover turned to Tim. "I am

being sorry that I cannot help you, Mr Diamond." His English was terrible, although his breath was worse. "Right now, you see, Mrs Lee and I are closing down Dream Time, so if you have come about your little brother…"

"I don't need charity," I said.

"We helped a boy like you just a month ago," Fiona Lee said. She blinked, and her eyelashes seemed to wave goodbye. "He had always wanted to climb mountains, but he was afraid of heights."

"So did you buy him a small mountain?" Tim asked.

"No. We got him help from a psychiatrist. Then we paid for him to fly to Mount Everest. That little boy went all the way to the top! And although he unfortunately fell off, he was happy. That is the point of our work, Mr Diamond. We use the money that we raise to make children happy."

"And take the case of Billy!" Hoover added. He pointed at yet another photograph on the wall. If Dream Time had helped many more kids, they'd have run out of wall. "Billy was a boy who wanted to be a dancer. He was being bullied at school. So we hired some bullies to bully the bullies for Billy and now, you see, Billy is in the ballet!"

"Bully for Billy," I muttered.

"So how can we be of helping to you, Mr Diamond?" Hoover asked.

"I have some questions," Tim said. "About a friend of yours called Lenny Smile."

Both Rodney Hoover and Fiona Lee froze. Hoover licked his teeth, which can't have been a lot of fun. Fiona had gone pale. Even her make-up seemed to have lost some of its colour. "Why are you asking questions about Lenny?" she asked.

"Because that way people give me answers," Tim replied. "It's what I do. I'm a private detective."

There was an ugly silence. I had to say that it suited Rodney Hoover.

"Lenny is dead," he said. "You know very well that he's lying there in Brompton Cemetery. Yes? What could you possibly want to know about him?"

"I know he's dead," Tim said. "But I'd be interested to know exactly how he died. I understand you were there."

"We were there," Fiona said. A single tear had appeared in the corner of her eye and began to trickle down her cheek. "Poor, poor Lenny! It was the most ghastly, horrible moment in my life, Mr Diamond."

"I don't suppose it was a terrific moment for him either," I muttered.

She ignored me. "It was about eleven o'clock. Mr Hoover and myself had gone to see him. He didn't like to come out of his flat, so we often went round there to tell him how much money we had raised and how the charity was progressing. We talked. We had a glass of wine. And then we left."

"Lenny said he would come down with us to the car," Hoover continued. "It was a very beautiful night. He wanted to have some of the fresh air ... you know? And so, we left the flat together."

"Lenny was a little bit ahead of us," Fiona Lee explained. "He was a fast walker. Mr Hoover stopped to tie his shoelaces and I waited for him. Lenny stepped into the road. And then..."

"The steamroller was going too fast." He swore quietly in a foreign language. Fiona sighed. "But the driver was on his way home. He was in the hurry. And he ran over Lenny!" He shook his head. "There was nothing, nothing we could do!"

"Do you know the driver's name?" Tim asked.

"I believe it is Krishner. Barry Krishner."

"Do you know what happened to him?"

"He is in a hospital for the hopelessly insane in north London ... in Harrow," Fiona said. "You can imagine that it was a dreadful experience for him, running over a man with a steamroller. But it was his fault! And because he was speeding, he killed one of the most wonderful men who ever lived. Lenny Smile! I had worked for him for twenty years. Mr

Hoover too."

"You'd only worked for him for two years?" Tim asked.

"No. I worked with him also for twenty years," Hoover said. "But are you telling me, please, Mr Diamond. Who hired you to ask these questions about Lenny Smile?"

"I never reveal the names of my clients," Tim replied. "Joe Carter wants to remain anonymous."

"Carter!" Hoover muttered. He gave Tim an ugly look. It wasn't difficult. "I could have guessed this. Yes! He came here, asking all his questions as if Fiona and me..." He stopped himself. "There was not one thing suspicious about his death, Mr Diamond. It was an accident. We know. Why? Because we were there! You think someone killed him? Poppycock! Who would wish to kill him?"

"Maybe he had enemies," Tim said.

"Everybody loved Lenny," Fiona retorted. "Even his enemies loved him. All he did his whole life was give away money and help young people. That man built so many orphanages, we had to advertise for orphans to fill them."

"What else can you tell us about him?" I asked.

"It's hard to describe Lenny to someone who never met him."

"Try. Where did he live?"

"He rented a flat in Welles Road. Number seventeen. He didn't buy anywhere because he hated spending money on himself." She took out a tiny handkerchief and dabbed the corner of her eye. "It is true that he liked to be on his own a lot."

"Why?"

"Because of his allergies."

I remembered now. Carter had said he was sick.

"What was he allergic to?" I asked.

"Many, many things," Hoover replied. "Chocolate, peanuts, yoghurt, animals, elastic bands, insects…"

"If he was stung by a wasp, he would be in hospital for a week," Fiona agreed.

"He was also allergic to hospitals. He had to go to a private clinic." Hoover stood up. Suddenly the interview was over. "Lenny Smile was a very unique man. He was – as you say – one in a million. And you have no right … no right to come here like this. You are wrong! Wrong with all your suspiciousness."

"Yes." Fiona nodded in agreement. "His death was a terrible accident. But the police investigated. They found nothing. Mr Hoover and I were there and we saw nothing."

"You can say to your 'anonymous' client, Mr Carter, that he should go back to Chicago," Hoover concluded. "And now, please, I think you should leave."

29

We left. The last thing I saw was Rodney Hoover standing next to Fiona Lee. The two of them were holding hands. Were they just co-workers, friends ... or something more? And there was something else. Hoover had said something. I wasn't sure what it was, but I was certain he had told me something that in fact he didn't want me to know. I tried to play back the conversation but it wouldn't come.

Tim and I left the offices of Dream Time together. Rodney Hoover and Fiona Lee had given us both the creeps. Neither of us said anything. But we both looked very carefully before we crossed the road.

At least Fiona had given us Smile's address, and as it wasn't far away that was where we went next.

Welles Road was round the back of Battersea, not far from the famous dogs' home. The tall, red-bricked buildings were all mansion flats ... not as big as mansions, but certainly smarter than your average flat. There were a dozen people living in each block, with their names listed on the front door. It turned out that Smile had lived at 17A – on the fifth floor. We rang the bell, but there was no answer so we tried 17B. There was a pause, then a woman's voice crackled over the intercom.

"Who is it?"

"We're friends of Lenny Smile," I shouted

back before Tim could come up with a story of his own.

"The fifth floor!" the voice called out. There was a buzz and the door opened.

With its faded wallpaper and worn carpets, the building seemed somehow tired inside. And so were we by the time we got to the fifth floor. The lift wasn't working. The whole place smelled of damp and yesterday's cooking. I thought you needed to be rich to live in Battersea (unless, of course, you happened to be a dog). But anyone could have lived here if they weren't fussy. The fifth floor was also the top floor. The door of 17B was open when we arrived.

"Mr Smile is dead!"

The woman who had broken the news to us so discreetly was about eighty, with white hair that might have been a wig and a face that had long ago given up trying to look human. Her eyes, nose and mouth all seemed to have run into each other like a melting candle. Her voice was still crackling, even without the intercom system. She was dressed in a pale orange dress decorated with flowers; the sort of material that would have looked better on a chair. There were fluffy pink slippers on her feet. Her legs – what I could see of them – were stout and hairy and made me glad that I couldn't see more.

"Who are you?" Tim asked.

"My name's Lovely."

"I'm sure it is," Tim agreed. "But what is it?"

"I just told you, dear. Lovely! Rita Lovely! I live next door to Mr Smile. Or at least … I used to."

"Have you moved?" Tim asked.

Mrs Lovely blinked at him. "No. Don't be daft! Mr Smile is the one who's moved. All the way to Brompton Cemetery!"

"We know that," Tim said. "We've already been there."

"Then what do you want?"

"We want to get into his flat."

"Why?"

I decided it was time to take over. "Mr Smile was my hero," I lied. I'd put on the little-boy-lost look that usually worked with very old women. And also, for that matter, with Tim. "He helped me."

"He gave you money?" She looked at me suspiciously.

"He saved my life. I had a rare disease."

"What disease?"

"It was so rare, it didn't have a name. Mr Smile paid for my medicine. I never got a chance to thank him. And I thought, if I could at least see where he lived…"

That softened her. "I've got a key," she said, taking it out of her pocket. "I was his neighbour for seven years and I used to look after the place for him when he was away. You seem a nice boy, so I'll let you in, just for a few minutes. This way…"

It seemed to take her for ever to reach the door, but then she was very old. At last we were in. Mrs Lovely closed the door behind us and sat down to have a rest.

Smile's flat was small and ordinary. There was a living-room, but it was so neat and impersonal that it was hard to believe anyone had done any living there at all. There was a three-piece suite, a coffee table, a few ornaments. The pictures on the wall were even less interesting than the walls they hung on. It was the same story in the other rooms. The flat told us nothing about the person who had lived there. Even the fridge was empty.

"How often did you see Mr Smile?" I asked.

"I never saw him," Tim replied.

"I know, Tim. I'm asking Mrs Lovely."

"I hardly ever saw him," Mrs Lovely said. "He kept himself to himself, if you want the truth. Although I was here the night that he got run over."

"Did you see what happened?"

"Not really, no." She shook her head vigorously and then readjusted her hair and teeth. "But I did see him go out. There were two people with him, talking to him. They seemed to be helping him down the stairs."

"Helping him?"

33

"One on each side of him. A man and a woman…"

That would have been Rodney Hoover and Fiona Lee.

"After they'd gone, I heard the most terrible noise. It was a sort of rumble and then a scrunching. At first I thought it was my indigestion, but then I looked out of the window. And there they were! The two of them and the driver—"

"Barry Krishner…"

"I don't know his name, young man. But yes, the driver of the steamroller was there. He was looking as sick as a parrot. Hardly surprising!"

"What happened to the parrot?" Tim asked.

"There was no parrot!"

"You mean … it got so sick it died?"

"There was the driver, the two people I had seen on the stairs and blood all over the road!" Mrs Lovely sighed. "It was the worst thing I have ever seen, and I've lived through two world wars! Blood everywhere! Lots and lots and lots of blood…"

"Thank you," Tim interrupted, going pale.

"Were there no other witnesses?" I asked.

"Just one." Mrs Lovely leant forward. "There was a balloon-seller on the other side of the road. He must have seen everything. I've already been asked about him once, so before you ask me again let me tell you that I don't know his name or where he had come from. He was an old man. He had a beard and about fifty helium balloons. Floating above his head."

"Why was his beard floating over his head?" Tim asked.

"The balloons, Tim!" I growled. I turned to Mrs Lovely. "Is there anything else you can tell us?" I asked. "Anything about Lenny Smile?"

"No. Not really." Suddenly there were tears in the old woman's eyes. She took out a handkerchief and blew her nose loudly. "I will miss him. It's true I hardly ever saw him, but he was a gentleman. Look at this note he sent me. It was my ninety-first birthday last week and he slipped it under the door."

She produced a crumpled sheet of paper, torn out of an exercise book. There were a couple of lines written in green ink:

Dear Mrs Lovely,
I hope you have a lovely birthday.
L.S.

That was all. The note couldn't have been less interesting or informative. And yet even so I thought there was something strange about it, something that didn't quite add up. I handed it back.

"Nobody else remembered my birthday," Mrs Lovely sighed. "I didn't get any cards. But then, most of my friends were blown up in the war…" She wiped her eyes. "I couldn't have asked for a more quiet neighbour," she said. "And now that he's gone, I'll really miss him."

How could she miss him when she had hardly ever met him? And why had Lenny Smile taken so much care not to be seen? I was beginning to realize that it wasn't just Carter's photograph that had been blurred. The same thing could be said for everything in Lenny Smile's life.

We found Barry Krishner, the steamroller driver, easily enough. There was only one institute for the hopelessly insane in Harrow. Well, two if you count the famous public school which was just a little further down the road. The hospital was a big, Victorian building, set in its own grounds with a path leading up to the front door.

"Are you sure this is the right place?" Tim asked.

"Yes," I said. "They've even got crazy paving."

I have to say, I was a bit worried about going into a mental asylum with Tim. I wondered if they'd let him out again. But it was too late to back out now. One of the doctors, a man called Eams, was waiting for us at the entrance. He was a short man, bald with a little beard that could have been bought at a joke shop. We introduced ourselves and he led us out of the winter sunlight into the gloomy heart of the building.

"Krishner has responded very well to treatment," he said. "Otherwise I would not let you speak with him. Even so, I must ask you to be extremely careful. As I am sure you can imagine, running someone over with a steamroller would be a very upsetting experience."

"For Lenny Smile?" Tim asked.

"For the driver! When Krishner first came here, he was in a state of shock. He ate very little. He barely spoke. Every night he woke up screaming."

"Bad dreams, Dr Eams?" Tim asked.

"Yes. But we have given him a lot of therapy and there has been considerable improvement. However, please, Mr Diamond, try not to refer to what happened. Don't mention any of the details – the steamroller, the accident itself. You have to be discreet!"

"Discreet is my middle name!" Tim nodded.

"And also please bear in mind, he is not a lunatic. He is here as my patient. So don't say anything that would make him think he is mentally ill."

Tim laughed. "I'd be mad to do that!" He nudged the doctor. "So, where's his padded cell?"

Barry Krishner was sitting in a small, old-fashioned room that could just as easily have belonged to a seaside hotel as an asylum. A large window looked out onto the garden and there were no bars. He was a small, grey-haired man, dressed in an old sports jacket and dark trousers. I noticed his eyes blinked a lot behind his spectacles, and he kept on picking his nails. Otherwise it would have been impossible to tell that he had, until recently, been in shock.

"Good afternoon, Barry," Dr Eams said. "These people want to ask you some very important questions about Lenny Smile." Krishner twitched as if he had just been electrocuted. Dr Eams smiled and continued in a soothing tone of voice. "You have nothing to worry about. They're not going to upset you." He nodded at Tim.

"It must have been a crushing experience," Tim began.

Krishner whimpered and twisted in his chair. Dr Eams frowned at Tim, then gently took hold of Krishner's arm. "Are you all right, Barry?" he asked. "Would you like me to get you a drink?"

"Good idea," Tim agreed. "Why not have a squash?"

Krishner shrieked. His glasses had slipped off his nose and one of his eyes had gone bloodshot.

"Mr Diamond!" Eams was angry now. "Please could you be careful what you say.

You told me you were going to ask Barry what he saw outside Lenny Smile's house."

"Flat," Tim corrected him.

Krishner went completely white. I thought he was going to pass out.

Dr Eams stared at Tim. "For heaven's sake…!" he rasped.

"OK, doc." Tim winked. "I think it's time we got to the crunch…"

Krishner began to foam at the mouth.

"I really want to crack this case. Although I have to say, the clues are a bit thin on the ground…"

Barry Krishner screamed and jumped out of the window. Without opening it. Alarms went off all over the hospital and, two minutes later, Tim and I were being escorted off the premises with the gates locked securely behind us.

"They weren't very helpful," Tim muttered. "Do you think it was something I said?"

I didn't answer. We had spent the whole day following in a supposedly dead man's footsteps. They had led us nowhere.

So where did we go now?

A NIGHT
AT THE CIRCUS

The next day was a Saturday. Tim was in a bad mood when he came in for breakfast. He'd obviously got out of bed the wrong side: not a good idea, since he slept next to the window. At least there was food in the fridge. The money that Joe Carter had paid us would last us a month, and that morning I'd cooked up eggs, bacon, tomatoes, sausages and beans. The papers had arrived – the *Sun* for me, the *Dandy* for Tim. An hour later the two of us were so full we could barely move. There's nothing like a great British breakfast for a great British heart attack.

But the truth is, we were both down in the dumps – and this time I don't mean the flat. We were no nearer to finding the truth about Smile. Rodney Hoover and Fiona Lee, the pair who ran Dream Time, were obviously creepy. According to Mrs Lovely, the next-door neighbour, they had half-carried Smile down-stairs just before his fatal accident. Had he been drunk? Or drugged? They could have thrown him in front of the steamroller – but if so, why? As Tim would doubtless have said, they'd have needed a pressing reason.

Barry Krishner, the driver of the steamroller, hadn't been able to tell us anything. After his encounter with Tim, it would probably be years before he talked again. He might babble and jibber, but I guessed talking would be a little beyond him. The police had presumably investigated and found nothing. Maybe there was nothing to find.

And yet...

Part of me still wondered if Lenny Smile really was dead. I remembered the man I had glimpsed in Brompton Cemetery. He had looked remarkably like the man I had seen in the photograph, and had certainly taken off fast enough when I spotted him. But if Lenny wasn't dead, where was he? And who was it who had disappeared under the steamroller?

"I give up!" Tim exclaimed.

He seemed to be reading my mind. "This isn't an easy case," I agreed.

"No!" He pointed. "I'm talking about this crossword in the *Dandy*!"

I ignored him and flicked over the page in my newspaper. And that was when I saw it. It was on the same page as the horoscopes. An advertisement for a circus in Battersea Park.

Direct from Moscow
THE RUSSIAN STATE CIRCUS
Starring
The Flying Karamazov Brothers
Karl "On Your" Marx – The Human Cannon-ball
The Fabulous Tina Trotsky
Three Sisters on Unicycles
And much, much more!

There was a picture showing a big top, but it was what was in front that had caught my eye. It was a figure in silhouette. A man selling balloons.

"Look at this, Tim!" I exclaimed, sliding the newspaper towards him.

Tim quickly read the page. "That's amazing!" he said. "I'm going to meet an old friend!"

"What are you talking about?"

"My horoscope. That's what it says…"

"Not the horoscopes, Tim! Look at the advertisement underneath!"

Tim read it. "This is no time to be going to the circus, Nick," he said. "We're on a case!"

"But look at the balloon-seller!" I took a deep breath. "Don't you remember what Mrs Lovely said? There was a witness when Lenny Smile was killed. It was a man selling balloons. I thought that was odd at the time. Why should there have been a balloon-seller in Battersea Park in the middle of the night?"

"He could have been lost…"

"I don't think so. I think he must have been part of the circus. There's a picture of him here in the paper. Maybe the balloon-seller was advertising the circus!"

"You mean … on his balloons?"

"Brilliant, Tim! Got it in one."

Tim ripped the page of the newspaper in half. He must have accidentally caught hold of the tablecloth, because he ripped that in half too. He folded the paper into his top pocket. "It's your turn to do the washing-up," he said. "Then let's go!"

In fact we didn't go back to Battersea until that evening. According to the advertisement, there was only one performance of the circus that day – at seven thirty – and I didn't see any point in turning up before. If the balloon-seller really was part of the big top, he'd probably be somewhere around during the performance. We would catch up with him then.

I don't know what you think about circuses. To be honest, I've never been a big fan. When you really think about it, is there anybody in the world less funny than a clown? And what can you say about somebody who has spent half their life learning how to balance thirty spinning plates and an umbrella on their nose?

OK. It's clever. But there simply have to be more useful things to do with your time! And, for that matter, with your nose. There was a time when they used to have animals – lions and elephants – performing in the ring. They were banned and I have to agree that was a good idea. But for my money they could ban the rest of the performers too, and put everyone out of their misery. I'm sorry. I've heard of people who have run away to join a circus, but speaking personally I'd run away to avoid seeing one.

But that said, I had to admit that the Russian State Circus looked interesting. It had parked its tent right in the middle of the park and there was something crazy and old-fashioned about the bright colours and the fluttering flags all edged silver by a perfect November moon. Four or five hundred people had turned out to see the show, and there were stilt-walkers and jugglers keeping the lines amused as they queued up to get in. As well as the tent itself there were about a dozen caravans parked on the grass, forming a miniature town. Some of these were modern and ugly. But there were also wooden caravans, painted red, blue and gold, that made me think of Russian gypsies and Russian palm-readers – old crones telling your future by candlelight. Tim had had his palm read once, when we were in Torquay. The palm-reader had laughed so much she'd had to lie down ... and that was only the contents of one finger on his left hand.

We bought tickets for the show. Tim wanted to see it, and having come all this way across London, I thought why not? We bought two of the last seats and followed the crowd in. Somehow the tent seemed even bigger inside than out. It was lit by flaming torches on striped, wooden poles. Grey smoke coiled in the air and dark shadows flickered across the ring. The whole place was bathed in a strange, red glow that seemed to transport us back to another century. The top of the tent was a tangle of ropes and wires, of rings and trapezes, all promises of things to come, but right now the ring was empty. There were wooden benches raked up in a steep bank, seven rows deep, forming a circle all round the sawdust. We were in the cheapest seats, one row from the back. As a treat, I'd bought Tim a stick of candyfloss. By the time the show started, he'd managed to get it all over himself as well as about half a dozen people on either side.

A band took its place on the far side of the ring. There were five players, dressed in old, shabby tailcoats. They had faces to match. The conductor looked about a hundred years old. I just hoped the music wouldn't get too exciting – I doubted his heart would stand it. With a trembling hand, he raised his baton and the band began to play. Unfortunately, the players all began at different times and what followed was a tremendous wailing and screeching as they all raced to get to the end first. But the conductor didn't seem to notice and the audience loved it. They'd come out for a good time and even when the violinist fell off his chair and the trombonist dropped his trombone they cheered and applauded.

By now I was almost looking forward to seeing the show ... but as things turned out, we weren't going to see anything of the performance that night.

The band came to the end of its first piece and began its second – which could have been either a new piece or the same piece played again. It was hard to be sure. I was glancing at the audience when suddenly I froze. There was a man sitting in the front row, right next to the gap in the tent where the performers would come in. He was wearing a dark coat, a hat and gloves. He was too far away. Or maybe it was the poor light or the smoke. But once again his face was blurred. Even so, I knew him at once.

It was the man from the Brompton Cemetery.

The man in the photograph at the Café Debussy.

Lenny Smile!

I grabbed hold of Tim. "Quick!" I exclaimed.

"What is it?" Tim jerked away, propelling

the rest of his candyfloss off the end of his stick and into the lap of the woman behind him.

"There!" I pointed. But even as I searched for Lenny across the crowded circus, I saw him get up and slip out into the night. By the time Tim had followed my finger to the other side of the tent, he had gone.

"Is it a clown?" Tim asked.

"No, Tim! It's the blurred man!"

"Who?"

"Never mind. We've got to go…"

"But the circus hasn't even begun!"

I dragged Tim to his feet and we made our way to the end of the row and out of the big top. My mind was racing. I still didn't know who the man in the dark coat really was. But if it was the same person I had seen at the cemetery, what was he doing here? Could he perhaps have followed us? No – that was impossible. I was sure he hadn't seen us across the crowded auditorium. He was here for another reason, and somehow I knew it had nothing to do with spinning plates and custard pies.

We left the tent just as the ringmaster, a tall man in a bright red jacket and black top hat, arrived to introduce the show. I heard him bark out a few words in Russian, but by then Tim and I were in the open air with the moon high above us, the park eerie and empty and the caravans clustered together about thirty metres away.

"What is it?" Tim demanded. He had forgotten why we had come and was disappointed to be missing the show.

Quickly I told him what I had seen. "We've got to look for him!" I said.

"But we don't know where he is!"

"That's why we've got to look for him."

There seemed to be only one place he could have gone. We went over to the caravans, suddenly aware how cold and quiet it was out here, away from the crowds. The first caravan was empty. The second contained a dwarf sipping sadly at a bottle of vodka. As we made our way over to the third, a man dressed in a fake leopard skin walked past carrying a steel girder. Inside the tent I heard the ringmaster come to the end of a sentence and there was a round of applause. Either he had cracked a joke or the audience was just grateful he'd stopped talking. There was a drum roll. We approached the fourth caravan.

Lenny Smile – if that's who it was – had disappeared. But there was another dead man in Battersea Park that night.

I saw the balloons first and knew at once whose caravan this was. There were more than fifty of them, every colour imaginable, clinging together as if they were somehow alive and knew what had just happened. The strange thing was that they did almost seem to be cowering in the corner. They weren't touching the ground. But the balloon-seller was. He was stretched out on the carpet with something silver lying next to his outstretched hand.

"Don't touch it, Tim!" I warned.

Too late. Tim had already leaned over and picked it up.

It was a knife. The blade was about ten centimetres long. It matched, perfectly, the ten-centimetre deep wound in the back of the balloon-seller's head. There wasn't a lot of blood. The balloon-seller had been an old man. Killing him had been like attacking a scarecrow.

And then somebody screamed.

I spun round. There was a little girl there in a gold dress with sequins. She was sitting on a bicycle which had only one wheel, pedalling back and forth to stop herself falling over. She was pointing at Tim, her finger trembling, her eyes filled with horror, and suddenly I was aware of the other performers appearing, coming out of their caravans as if this was the morning and they'd just woken up. Only it was the middle of the night and these people weren't dressed for bed! There was a clown in striped pants with a bowler hat and (inevitably) a red nose. There was a man on stilts. A fat man with a crash helmet. Two more sisters on unicycles. The strong man had come back with his steel girder. A pair of identical twins stood like mirror images, identical expressions on their faces. And what they were all looking at was my big brother Tim, holding a knife and hovering in the doorway of a man who had just been murdered.

The little girl who had started it screamed once more and shouted something out. The strong man spoke. Then the clown. It all came out as jibberish to me but it didn't take a lot of imagination to work out what they were saying.

"*Boris the balloon man has been murdered!*"

"*Dear old Boris! Who did it?*"

"*It must have been the idiotic-looking Englishman holding the knife.*"

I don't know at what precise moment the mood turned nasty, but suddenly I realized that the people all around me no longer wanted to entertain us. The clown stepped forward and his face was twisted and ugly ... as well as being painted white with green diamonds over his eyes. He asked Tim something, his voice cracking with emotion and his make-up doing much the same.

"I don't speak Russian," Tim said.

"You kill Boris!"

So the balloon man really was called Boris. The clown was speaking English with an incredibly thick accent, struggling to make himself understood.

"Me?" Tim smiled and innocently raised a hand. Unfortunately it was the hand that was still holding the knife.

"Why you kill Boris?"

"Actually, I think you mean 'why *did* you kill Boris,'" Tim corrected him. "You've forgotten the verb…"

"I don't think they want an English lesson, Tim," I said.

Tim ignored me. "I kill Boris, you kill Boris, he killed Boris!" he explained to the increasingly puzzled clown.

"I didn't kill Boris!" I exclaimed.

"They killed Boris!" the clown said.

"That's right!" Tim smiled encouragingly.

"No, we didn't!" I yelled.

It was too late. The circus performers were getting closer by the second. I didn't like the way they were looking at us. And there were more of them now. Four muscle-bound brothers in white leotards had stepped out of the shadows. The ringmaster was staring at us from the edge of the tent. I wondered who was entertaining the audience. The entire circus seemed to have congregated outside.

The ringmaster snapped out a brief command in Russian.

"Let's go, Tim!" I said.

Tim dropped the knife and we turned and fled just as the performers started towards us. As far as they were concerned, Tim had just murdered one of their number, and this was a case of an eye for an eye – or a knife wound for a knife wound. These were travelling performers.

They had their own rules and to hell with the country in which they found themselves.

Tim and I took off across the park, trying to lose ourselves in the shadows. Not easy with a full moon that night. Something huge and solid sailed across the sky, then buried itself in the soft earth. The strong man had thrown his girder in our direction. We were lucky – he was strong, but he obviously had lousy aim. The girder would be found the next day sticking out of the grass like a bizarre, iron tree. Half a metre to the right and we'd have been found underneath it.

But I quickly realized that this was only the start of our troubles. The entire circus troupe had abandoned the performance in order to come after us. Word had quickly got round. We had killed old Boris and now they were going to kill us. There was a dull *whoomph!* and a figure shot through the air. It was the man in the crash helmet. This had to be Karl "On Your" Marx, the human cannon-ball. They had fired him in our direction, and I just had time to glimpse his outstretched fists as he soared through the night sky before I grabbed hold of Tim and threw him onto the grass. Marx whizzed past. We had been standing in front of an oak tree and there was a dull crunch as he hit the trunk, ending up wedged in a fork in the branches.

"Do you think he's OK?" Tim asked.

"I don't think he's oak anything!" I replied. "Come on!"

We scrabbled to our feet just as the clown set off across the grass, speeding towards us in a tiny, multicoloured car. I looked ahead with a sinking heart. We really were in the middle of nowhere, with grass all around, the river in the far distance and nobody else in sight. Anybody who had come to the park at that time of night would now be in the circus, watching the show.

"Run, Tim!" I gasped.

The clown was getting nearer. I could see his face, even less funny than usual, the grease paint livid in the moonlight. In seconds he would catch up with us and run us down. But then there was an explosion. The bonnet of the car blew open, the wheels fell off, water jetted off the radiator and smoke billowed out of the boot. The clown must have pressed the wrong button. Either that, or the car had done what it was designed for.

"Which way?" Tim panted.

I turned and looked back. For a brief, happy moment, I thought we had left the circus folk behind us, but then something whizzed through the darkness and slammed into the bark of another tree. It was a knife – but thrown from where? I looked up. There was a long telephone wire crossing the park, connected to a series of poles. And, impossibly, a man was standing, ten metres above the ground, reaching for a second knife. It was a tightrope walker. He had followed us along the telephone wires and was there now, balancing effortlessly in mid-air. At the same time, I heard the sudden cough of an engine and saw a motorbike lurch across the lawn. It was being driven by one of the brothers in white leotards. He had two more brothers standing on his shoulders. The fourth brother was on top of the other two brothers, holding what looked horribly like an automatic machine-gun. The motorbike rumbled towards us, moving slowly because of the weight of the passengers. But as I watched, it was overtaken by the three sisters on their unicycles. The moonlight sparkled not only on their sequins but on the huge swords which one of the other performers must have given them. All three of them were yelling in high-pitched voices, and somehow I knew that I wasn't hearing a Russian folk song. The man on stilts came striding towards us, moving like some monstrous insect, throwing impossibly long shadows across the grass. Somehow he had got ahead of us. And finally, to my astonishment, there was a sudden bellow and a full-sized adult elephant came lumbering out of the trees with a girl in white feathers sitting astride its neck. This would have to be the lovely Tina Trotsky. And despite the law, the Russian State Circus did have an animal or two hidden in its big top.

They had an elephant! Did they also, I wondered, have lions?

Tim had seen it too. "They've got an elephant!" he exclaimed.

"I've seen it, Tim!"

"Is it African or Indian?"

"What?"

"I can never remember which is which!"

"What does it matter?" I almost screamed the words. "It won't make any difference when it stamps on us!"

The circus performers were closing in on us from all sides. There was a rattle from the machine-gun and bullets tore into the ground, ripping up the grass. The dwarf I had seen in the caravan had woken up. It now turned out he was a fire-eating dwarf ... at least, that might explain the flame-thrower he had strapped to his back. We had the elephant, the motorbike and the unicycles on one side. The dwarf and the stilt man were on the other. The tightrope walker was still somewhere overhead. The human cannon-ball was disentangling himself from the tree.

Things weren't looking good.

But then a car suddenly appeared, speeding across the grass. It raced past one of the unicyclists, knocking her out of the way, then curved round, snapping the stilt man's stilts in half. The stilt man yelled and dived head first into a bank of nettles. The elephant fell back, rearing up. Tina Trotsky somersaulted backwards, feathers fluttering all around her. The car skidded to a halt next to us and a door swung open.

"Get in!" someone said, and already I knew that I recognized the voice.

"Are you a taxi?" Tim asked. I think he was worrying about the fare.

"It doesn't matter what it is, Tim," I said. "Just get in!"

I pushed Tim ahead of me and dived onto the back seat. There was another rattle of machine-gun fire, a burst of flame and a loud thud as a second knife slammed into the side of the door. But then the car was moving, bouncing up and down along the grass. I saw a bush blocking the way, right in front of us. The driver went straight through it. There was a road on the other side. A van swerved to avoid us as our tyres hit concrete, and a bus swerved to avoid the van. I heard the screech of tyres and the even louder screech of the drivers. There was the sound of crumpling metal. A horn blared.

But then we were away, leaving Battersea Park far behind us.

It's like I said. I'd never liked the circus. And the events of the night had done nothing to change my mind.

THE REAL
LENNY SMILE

"Well, well, well. This is a very nasty surprise. The Diamond brothers! Having a night at the circus?"

It was the driver of the car, the man who had saved us, who was speaking. He had driven us directly to his office at New Scotland Yard. It had been a while since we had last seen Detective Chief Inspector Snape. But here he was, as large as life and much less enjoyable.

It had been Snape who had once employed Tim as a police-constable. He had been no more than an inspector then – and he'd probably had far fewer grey hairs. He was a big, solid man who obviously worked out in a gym. Nobody got born with muscles like his. He had small blue eyes and skin the colour of raw ham. He was wearing a made-to-measure suit but unfortunately it had been made to measure somebody else. It looked as if it was about to burst. His tie was crooked. So were his teeth. So were most of the people he met.

I had never known his name was Freddy but that was what was written on the door. He had an office on the fourth floor, overlooking the famous revolving sign. I had been involved with Snape twice before: once when we were on the trail of the Falcon, and once when he had forced me to share a cell with the master criminal, Johnny Powers*. He wasn't someone I'd been looking forward to meeting a third time – even if he had just rescued us from the murderous crowd at the Russian State Circus.

His assistant was with him. Detective Superintendent Boyle hadn't changed much since the last time I'd seen him either. *His* first name must have been "Push". That was what was written on his door. Short and fat with curly black hair, he'd have done well in one of those BBC documentaries about Neanderthal man. He was wearing a black leather jacket and faded jeans. As usual he had a couple of medallions buried in the forest of hair that sprouted up his chest and out of his open-necked shirt. Boyle looked more criminal than a criminal. He wasn't someone you'd want to meet on a dark night. He wasn't someone you'd want to meet at all.

"This is incredible!" Tim exclaimed. He turned to me. "You remember the horoscope

* See *Public Enemy Number Two*

in the newspaper! It said I was going to meet an old friend!"

"I'm not an old friend!" Snape exploded. "I hate you!"

"*I'd* like to get friendly with him," Boyle muttered. He took out a knuckleduster and slid it over his right fist. "Why don't you let the two of us go somewhere quiet, Chief...?"

"Forget it, Boyle!" Snape snapped. "And where did you get the knuckleduster? Have you been in the evidence room again?"

"It's mine!" Boyle protested.

"Well, put it away..."

Boyle slid the contraption off his hand and sulked.

Snape sat down behind his desk. Tim and I were sitting opposite him. We'd been waiting for him in the office for a couple of hours but he hadn't offered either of us so much as a cup of tea.

"What I want to know," he began, "is what the two of you were doing at the circus tonight. Why were the performers trying to kill you? And what happened to Boris the balloon-seller?"

"Someone killed him," I said.

"I know that, laddy. I've seen the body. Someone stuck a knife in him."

"Yeah." I nodded. "The circus people thought it was us."

"That's an easy enough mistake to make

when you two are involved." Snape smiled mirthlessly. "We went to the circus because we wanted to talk to the balloon-seller," he explained. "Luckily for you. But why were you interested in him? That's what I want to know."

"I wanted to buy a balloon," I said.

"Don't lie to me, Diamond! Not unless you want to spend a few minutes on your own with Boyle."

"Just one minute," Boyle pleaded. "Thirty seconds!"

"All right," I said. "We were interested in Lenny Smile."

"Ah!" Snape's eyes widened. Boyle looked disappointed. "Why?"

"We're working for a man called Joe Carter. He's American..."

"He thinks Lenny Smile was murdered," Tim said.

Snape nodded. "Of course Smile was murdered," he said. "And it was the best thing that ever happened to him. If I wasn't a policeman, I'd have been tempted to murder him myself."

Tim stared. "But he was a saint!" he burbled.

"He was a crook! Lenny Smile was the biggest crook in London! Boyle and I have been investigating him for months – and we'd have arrested him if he hadn't gone under that steamroller." Snape opened a drawer and took out a file as thick as a north London telephone directory. "This is the file on Lenny Smile," he said. "Where do you want me to begin?"

"How about at the beginning?" I suggested.

"All right. Lenny Smile set up a charity called Dream Time. He employed two assistants ... Rodney Hoover, who comes from the Ukraine. And Fiona Lee. She's from Sloane Square. We've investigated them, and as far as we can see they're in the clear. But Smile? He was a different matter. All the money passed through his bank account. He was in financial control. And half the money that went in, never came out."

"You mean ... he stole it?" I asked.

"Exactly. Millions of pounds that should have gone to poor children went into his own pocket. And when he did spend money on children, he got everything cheap. He provided hospitals with cheap X-ray machines that could only see halfway through. He provided schools with cheap books full of typing errrors. He took a bunch of children on a cheap adventure holiday."

"What's wrong with that?"

"It was in Afghanistan! Half the children still haven't come back! He bought headache pills that actually gave you a headache and food parcels where the parcels tasted better than the food. I'm telling you, Diamond, Lenny Smile was so crooked he makes an evening with Jack the Ripper sound like a nice idea! And I was this close to arresting him." Snape held his thumb and forefinger just millimetres apart. "I already had a full-time police officer watching his flat. It's like I say. We were just going to arrest him – but then he got killed."

"Suppose he isn't dead," I said.

Snape shook his head. "There were too many witnesses. Mrs Lovely, the woman who lived next door, saw him leave the flat. Hoover and Lee were with him. There was Barry Krishner, the driver. And Boris…"

"Wait a minute!" I interrupted. "Mrs Lovely didn't actually see anything. Barry Krishner has gone mad. I'm not sure Hoover and Lee can be trusted. And someone has just killed Boris." I remembered what Mrs Lovely had told us. "Mrs Lovely said that someone had been asking questions about the balloon-seller," I went on. "I thought she was talking about you … the police! But now I wonder if it wasn't someone else. The real killer, for example!" Snape stared at me. "I think Boris saw what really happened," I concluded. "And that was why he was killed."

"Who by?" Snape demanded.

"By Lenny Smile!"

There was a long silence. Snape looked doubtful. Boyle looked … well the same way Boyle always looks.

"What do you mean?" Snape demanded at length.

"It all makes sense. Lenny Smile knew that you were after him. You say you had a policeman watching his flat?"

Snape nodded. "Henderson. He's disappeared."

"Since when?"

"He vanished a week before the accident with the steamroller…"

"That was no accident!" I said. "Don't you get it, Snape? Smile knew he was cornered. You were closing in on him. And Joe Carter was coming over too. Carter wanted to know what had happened to all the millions he'd given Dream Time. So Smile had to disappear. He faked his own death, and right now he's somewhere in London. We've seen him! Twice!"

That made Snape sit up. "Where?"

"He was at the circus. He was in the crowd. We saw him about a minute before Boris was killed. And he was at the cemetery. Not underground – on top of it! I followed him and he ran away."

"How do you know it was Smile?" Snape asked.

"I don't. At least, I can't be sure. But I've seen a photograph of him and it looked the same."

"We don't know much about Smile," Snape

admitted. "Henderson was watching the flat, but he only saw him once. We know when he was born and when he died. But that's about all…"

"He didn't die. I'm telling you. Dig up the coffin and you'll probably find it's empty!"

Snape looked at Boyle, then back at me. Slowly, he nodded. "All right, laddy," he said. "Let's play it your way. But if you're wasting my time … it's your funeral!"

"There was no funeral," I said. "Lenny Smile isn't dead."

"Let's find out…"

I'll tell you now. There's one place you don't want to be at five past twelve on a black November night – and that's in a cemetery. The ground was so cold I could feel it all the way up to my knees, and every time I breathed the ice seemed to find its way into my skull. There were the four of us there – Snape, Boyle, Tim and myself – and now we'd been joined by another half-dozen police officers and workmen, two of whom were operating a mechanical digger that whined and groaned as it clawed at the frozen earth. Tim was whining and groaning too, as a matter of fact. I think he'd have preferred to have been in bed.

But maybe it wasn't just the weather that was managing to chill me. The whole thing was like a scene out of *Frankenstein*. You know the one – where Igor the deformed Hungarian servant has to climb into the grave and steal a human brain. Glancing at Boyle, I saw a distinct physical resemblance. I had to remind myself that two days ago I had been enjoying half-term and that the following day I would be back at school, with all the fun of double geography and French. In the meantime I had somehow stumbled into a horror film. I wondered what was going to turn up in the final reel.

The digger stabbed down. The earth shifted. Gradually the hole got deeper. There was a clunk – metal hitting wood – and two of the workmen climbed in to clear away the rest of the soil with spades. Snape moved forward.

I didn't watch as the coffin was opened. You have to remember that I was only fourteen years old, and if someone had made a film out of what was going on here I wouldn't even have been allowed to see it.

"Boyle!" Snape muttered the single word and the other man lowered himself into the hole. There was a pause. Then...

"Sir!"

Boyle was holding something. He passed it up to Snape. It was dark blue, shaped a bit like a bell, only paper thin. There was a silver disc squashed in the middle. It took me a few seconds to work out what it was. Then I realized. It was a police-constable's helmet. But one that had been flattened.

"Henderson!" Snape muttered.

There had been a police-constable watching Smile's flat. He had disappeared a week before the accident. His name had been Henderson.

And now we knew what had happened to him.

"Don't you see, Tim? It was Henderson who was killed. Not Lenny Smile!"

The two of us were back at our Camden flat. After our hours spent in the cemetery, we were too cold to go to bed. I'd made us both hot chocolate and Tim was wearing two pairs of pyjamas and two dressing-gowns, with a hot-water bottle clasped to his chest.

"But who killed him?"

"Lenny Smile."

"But what about Hoover? And the woman? They were there when it happened."

For once, Tim was right. Rodney Hoover and Fiona Lee must have been part of it. Snape had already gone to arrest them. The man they had helped down the stairs must have been Henderson. I had been right about that. He had been drugged. They had taken him out of the flat and thrown him into the road, just as Barry Krishner turned the corner on his way home...

And yet it wasn't going to be easy to prove. There were no witnesses. And until Smile was found, it was hard to see exactly what he could do. Suddenly I realized how clever Smile had been. The blurred man? He had been more than that. He had run Dream Time, he had stolen all the money, and he had remained virtually invisible.

"Nobody knew him." I said.

"Who?"

"Smile. Mrs Lovely never spoke to him. Joe Carter only wrote to him. We went to his flat and it was like he'd never actually lived there. Even Rodney Hoover and Fiona Lee couldn't tell us much about him."

Tim nodded. I yawned. It was two o'clock, way past my bedtime. And in just five and a half hours I'd be getting ready for school. Monday was going to be a long day.

"You'll have to go to the Ritz tomorrow," I said.

"Why?"

"To tell Joe Carter about his so-called best friend."

Tim sighed. "It's not going to be easy," he said. "He had this big idea about Lenny Smile when all the time he was someone else!"

I finished my hot chocolate and stood up. Then, suddenly, it hit me. "What did you just say?" I asked.

"I've forgotten." Tim was so tired he was forgetting what he was saying even as he said it.

"Someone else! That's exactly the point! Of course!"

There had been so many clues. The note in the cemetery. Mrs Lovely and the card Lenny had sent her. The gravestone. The photograph of Smile outside the Café Debussy. And Snape...

"We know when he was born..."

But it was only now, when I was almost too tired to move, that it came together. The truth. All of it.

The following morning, I didn't go to school. Instead I made two telephone calls, and then later on, just after ten o'clock, Tim and I set out for the final showdown.

It was time to meet Lenny Smile.

THE BIG WHEEL

The tube from Camden Town to Waterloo is direct on the Northern line – which was probably just as well. I'd only had about five hours' sleep, and I was so tired that the whole world seemed to be shimmering and moving in slow motion. Tim was just as bad. He had a terrible nightmare in which he was lowered, still standing up, into Lenny's grave – and woke up screaming. I suppose it wasn't too surprising. He'd fallen asleep on the escalator.

But the two of us had livened up a little by the time we'd reached the other end. The weather had taken a turn for the worse. The rain was sheeting down, sucking any colour or warmth out of the city. We had left Waterloo station behind us, making for the South Bank, a stretch of London that has trouble looking beautiful even on the sunniest day. This is where you'll find the National Theatre and the

National Film Theatre, both designed by architects with huge buckets of prefabricated cement. There weren't many people around. Just a few commuters struggling with umbrellas that the wind had turned inside out. Tim and I hurried forward without speaking. The rain lashed down, hit the concrete and bounced up again, wetting us twice.

I had made the telephone call just after breakfast.

"*Mrs Lee?*"

"*Yes. Who is this?*" Fiona Lee's clipped vowels had been instantly recognizable down the line.

"*This is Nick Diamond. Remember me?*"

A pause.

"*I want to meet with Lenny Smile.*"

A longer pause. Then, "*That's not possible. Lenny Smile is dead.*"

"*You're lying. You know where he is. I want to see the three of you. Hoover, Lenny and you. Eleven o'clock at the London Eye. And if you don't want me to go to the police, you'd better not be late.*"

You've probably seen the London Eye, the huge Ferris wheel they put up outside County Hall. It's one of the big surprises of modern London. Unlike the Millennium Dome, it has actually been a success. It opened on time. It worked. It didn't fall over. At the end of the millennium year they decided to keep it, and suddenly it was part of London – a brilliant silver circle at once huge and yet somehow fragile. Tim had taken me on it for my fourteenth birthday and we'd enjoyed the view so much we'd gone a second time. Well as they say, one good turn deserves another.

Not that we were going to see much today. The clouds were so low that the pods at the top almost seemed to disappear into them. You could see the Houses of Parliament on the other side of the river and, hazy in the distance, St Paul's. But that was about it. If there was a single day in the year when it wasn't worth paying ten pounds for the ride, this was it, which would explain why there were no crowds around when we approached: just Rodney Hoover and Fiona Lee, both of them wearing raincoats, waiting for us to arrive.

There was no sign of Lenny Smile, but I wasn't surprised. I had known he would never show up.

"Why are you calling us?" Hoover demanded. "First we have the police accusing us of terrible things. Then you, wanting to see Lenny. We don't know where Lenny is! As far as we know, he's dead..."

"Why don't we get out of the rain?" I suggested. "How about the wheel?" It seemed like a good idea. The rain was still bucketing down and there was nowhere else to go.

"After you, Mr Hoover..."

We bought tickets and climbed into the first compartment that came round. I wasn't surprised to find that there would only be the four of us in it for this turn of the wheel. The doors slid shut, and slowly – so slowly that we barely knew we were moving – we were carried up into the sky, into the driving rain.

There was a pause as if nobody knew quite what to say. Then Fiona broke the silence. "We already told that ghastly little policeman … Detective Chief Inspector Snape. Lenny was with us that day. He was killed by the steamroller. And it *is* Lenny buried in the cemetery."

"No it isn't," I said. "Lenny Smile is right here now. He's on the big wheel. Inside this compartment."

"Is he?" Tim looked under the seat. "I don't see him!"

"That's because you're not looking in the right place, Tim," I said. "But that was the whole idea. You said it yourself last night. We all thought Lenny Smile was one thing, but in fact he was something else."

"You are not making the lot of sense," Hoover said. His face, already dark to begin with, had gone darker. He was watching me with nervous eyes.

"I should have known from the start that there was something strange about Lenny Smile," I said. "Nothing about him added up. Nobody – except you – had ever seen him. And

72

everything about him was a lie."

"You mean ... his name wasn't Lenny Smile?" Tim asked.

"Lenny Smile never existed, Tim!" I explained. "He was a fantasy. I should have known when I saw the details on the gravestone. It said that he was born on 31st April 1955. But that was the first lie. There are only thirty days in April. 31st April doesn't exist!"

"It was a mistake..." Fiona muttered.

"Maybe. But then there was that photograph Carter showed us of 'Lenny' standing outside the Café Debussy. You told us that he was allergic to a lot of things, and one of those things was animals. But in the photograph there's a cat sitting between his feet – and he doesn't seem to care. The allergy business was a lie. But it was a clever one. It meant that he had a reason not to be seen. He had to stay indoors because he was ill..."

Centimetre by centimetre, the big wheel carried us further away from the ground. The rain was hammering against the glass. Looking out, I could barely see the buildings on the north bank of the river. There was Big Ben, but then the rain swept across it, turning it into a series of brown and white streaks.

Tim gaped. "So there was no Lenny Smile!" he exclaimed.

"That's right. Except when Hoover *pretended* to be Lenny Smile. Don't you see? He

73

rented the flat even though he never actually lived there. Occasionally he went in and out to make it look as if there was someone there. And of course it was Hoover who wrote that letter to Mrs Lovely."

"How do you know?"

"Because it was written in green ink. The message we saw in the card on Lenny's grave was also written in green ink – and it was the same handwriting. I should have seen from the start. It was Hoover we saw at the circus. And he was also there at Brompton Cemetery the day we visited the grave. I should have known it was him as soon as we met him at the Dream Time office."

"Why?" Tim asked.

"Because Hoover had never met us – but somehow he knew we'd been to Brompton Cemetery. Don't you remember what he said to us? 'You know very well that he's lying there in Brompton Cemetery.' Those were his exact words. But he only knew we knew because he knew who we were, and he knew who we were because he'd seen us!"

Tim scratched his head. "Could you say that last bit again?"

Fiona looked at me scornfully. "You're talking tommy-rot!" she said.

"Was Tommy part of this too?" Tim asked.

"Why would Rodney and I want to invent a man called Lenny Smile?" she continued, ignoring him.

"Because the two of you were stealing millions of pounds from Dream Time. You knew that eventually the police would catch up with you. And there was always the danger that someone like Joe Carter would come over from America to find out what was happening to his money. You were the brains behind the charity. You were the 'big wheels', if you like. But you needed someone to take the blame and then disappear. That was Lenny Smile. Henderson – the policeman – must have found out what was going on, so he had to die too. And that was your brilliant idea. You'd turn Henderson into Lenny Smile. He went under the steamroller and, as far as you were concerned, that was the end of the matter. Smile was dead. There was nothing left to investigate."

The pod was still moving up. There were a few pedestrians out on the South Bank. By now they were no more than dots.

"But now the police think Lenny Smile is alive," I went on. "That's why the two of you aren't in jail. They're looking for him. They don't have any proof against you. So the two of you are in the clear!"

Hoover had listened to all this in silence but now he smiled, his thin lips peeling back from his teeth. "You have it exactly right," he said. "Fiona and I are nobodies. We were just working for Lenny Smile. He is the real crook. And, as you say, they have no proof. Nobody has any proof."

"Hoover dressed up as Lenny Smile…" Tim was still trying to work it all out.

"Only once. For the photograph that Joe Carter requested. But he was wearing the same coat and the same gloves when we saw him – which is why we thought he was Lenny Smile. Both times, he was too far away for us to see his face. And, of course, in the photograph the face was purposely blurred." I turned to Rodney. "I'd be interested to know, though. What were you doing in the cemetery?"

Hoover shrugged. "I realized that the bloody fool of an undertaker had made a mistake with the date on the gravestone. I went there to put it right. When I saw you and your brother at the grave, I knew something was wrong. I have to admit, I panicked. And ran."

"And the circus…?"

"Mrs Lovely told us there had been a witness. I had to track him down and make sure he didn't talk."

"But it wouldn't have mattered if he'd talked," Tim said. "He was Russian! Nobody would have understood."

"I don't believe in taking chances," Rodney said. His hand had slid into his coat pocket. Why wasn't I surprised, when it came out, to see that it was holding a gun?

"He's got a gun!" Tim squealed.

"That's right, Tim," I said.

"You've been very clever," Hoover snarled. "But you haven't quite thought it through." He glanced out of the window. We had reached the top of the circle, as high up as the Ferris wheel went. Suddenly Hoover fired. The glass door smashed. Tim leapt. The rain came rushing in. "An unfortunate accident!" Hoover shouted above the howl of the wind. "The door malfunctioned. Somehow it broke. You and your brother fell out."

"No we didn't!" Tim whimpered.

"Anyway, by the time they've finished wiping you off the South Bank, Fiona and I will have disappeared. The money is in a nice little bank in Brazil. We'll move there. A beach house in Rio de Janeiro! We'll live a life of luxury."

"That money was meant for sick children!" I shouted. "Don't you have any shame at all?"

"I cannot afford shame!" He gestured with the gun, pointing at the shattered glass and the swirling rain. "Now which one of you is going to step out first?"

"He is!" Tim pointed at me.

"No, I'm not," I said. I turned back to Hoover. "It won't work, Hoover. Why don't you take a look in the next pod?"

Hoover's eyes narrowed. Fiona Lee went over to the window. There were about twenty people in the pod above us on the London Eye.

All of them were dressed in blue. "It's full of policemen!" she exclaimed. She went over to the other side. "And the one below us! That's full of police too!"

"It must be their day out!" Tim said.

"Forget it, Tim." It was my turn to smile. "You've been set up, Hoover. Every word you've said has been recorded. The pod's bugged. Your confession is on tape right now, and as soon as the ride is over you and Fiona will have another ride. To jail!"

Fiona had begun to tremble. Hoover's eyes twitched. His grip tightened on the gun. "Maybe I'll kill you anyway," he said. "Just for the fun of it..."

And that was when the helicopter appeared – a dark-blue police helicopter, its blades beating at the rain outside the broken window. It had come swooping out of the clouds and now hovered just a few metres away. I could see Snape in the passenger seat. Boyle was in the back, dressed in a flak jacket, cradling an automatic rifle. I just hoped he was pointing it at Hoover, not at Tim.

"Why do you think the police released you?" I shouted above the noise of the helicopter. "I rang Snape this morning and told him what I'd worked out and he asked me to meet you. You walked into a trap. He knew you'd feel safe up in the air, just the four of us. He wanted you to confess."

A second later there was a crackle and Snape's voice came, amplified, from the helicopter. "Put the gun down, Hoover! The pod is surrounded!"

Hoover swore in Ukrainian, and before I could stop him he had twisted round and fired at the helicopter.

I threw myself at Hoover.

He fired a second time. But his aim had gone wild. The bullet hit Fiona in the shoulder. She screamed and fell to her knees.

Hoover, with my hands at his throat, crashed into the window. This one didn't break. I heard the toughened glass clunk against his un-toughened skull. His eyes glazed and he slid to the ground.

I turned to Tim. "Are you all right, Tim?" I asked.

"Yes, I'm fine." He pointed past the helicopter. "Look! You can see Trafalgar Square!"

It took another fifteen minutes for the pod to reach the ground. At once we were surrounded by uniformed police officers. Hoover and Lee were dragged out. They'd spend a few days in hospital on their way to jail. The helicopter with Snape and Boyle in was nowhere to be seen. With a bit of luck a strong gust of wind would have blown it out of London and maybe into Essex. The trouble with those two was that no matter how many times we helped them, they'd never thank us. And I'd probably end up with a detention for missing a day of school.

"We'd better go to the Ritz," I said.

"For tea?" Tim asked.

"No, Tim. Joe Carter…"

The American was still waiting to hear about his best friend, Lenny Smile. I wasn't looking forward to breaking the bad news to him. Maybe I'd leave that to Tim. After all, discreet was his middle name.

It had stopped raining. Tim and I walked along the South Bank, leaving the London Eye behind us. There were workmen ahead of us, shovelling a rich, black ooze onto the surface of the road. On the pavement, a tramp stood with an upturned hat, playing some sort of plinky-plonk music on a strange instrument – a zither, I think. I found a pound coin and dropped it into the hat. Charity. That was how this had all begun.

"Ta!" the tramp said.

"Tar? Don't worry," Tim said. "I've seen it…"

We crossed the river, the sound of the zither fading into the distance behind.